# I am Kind

I want to be kind
like my Mom.
She is the kindest
person I know.

She helps Grandma work out.
They walk in the park.

They bend and stretch.

It is fun.

Mom helps strangers, too.
Once a week we go to our town's
community center.

# We bake and cook.

We serve the food
to hungry people.

Stan lives next door.
He hurt his arm
and can't garden.
I try to be kind.

I weed and water
his plants.

Stan thanks me with
some strawberries.

How kind!

When the rain comes down,
my umbrella goes up.

I find room
for one more
to be kind.

Maya is a new student
at my school.
Her family just moved to town.

She is my new math partner.

I see Maya
sitting alone at lunch.

My friends and I
ask her to eat with us.

She thanks us
for being kind.

At home
I like to build
big spaceships.

My baby brother likes
to knock them down.

Sometimes it isn't easy
to be kind.
But I find a way.

My troop goes on a nature hike.
Maya joins us.

First, we cross a creek.
We cheer for each other.

Next, we climb a winding path.
Some climb fast. Some climb slow.
I am kind to all.

We reach the campsite.
We take a break.
It's time to eat.
Yum!

We learn about plants and animals.

It is time to go home.
We pack up everything.
We clean up the site.

We are kind to the earth.

That night, Maya sleeps over.
I have an idea to be kind.
Maya likes it a lot.
We draw sketches.
We make lists.

We tell our plan
to my mom.

She loves it!

We borrow some
supplies from Stan.

He loves our idea, too.

We go shopping with my mom.
We buy a few more supplies.

We get to work.
I dig holes.
Maya plants the flowers.
We work hard.

At last, we are done. Now everyone
can enjoy our surprise.

It is the best feeling
when I am kind.

# How can
## YOU
### be kind?

# Can you think of
# three examples?